THE ENCHANTED SEA AND OTHER TALES

The Enchanted Sea
The Goldfish that Grew
The Goblin in the Train

Copyright © Darrell Waters Limited 1951
Copyright © illustrations Century Hutchinson Limited 1986
First published by Pitkin London 1951

Published in 1986 by Hutchinson Children's Books Ltd
An imprint of Century Hutchinson Ltd
Brookmount House, 62–65 Chandos Place, Covent Garden,
London WC2N 4NW

Century Hutchinson Publishing Group (Australia) Pty Ltd
16–22 Church Street, Hawthorn, Melbourne, Victoria 3122

Century Hutchinson Group (NZ) Ltd
32–34 View Road, PO Box 40–086, Glenfield, Auckland 10

Century Hutchinson Group (SA) Pty Ltd
PO Box 337, Bergvlei 2012, South Africa

Designed by Sarah Harwood
Edited by Sarah Ware

Set in Souvenir Light 774 12/14pt.
by Southern Positives and Negatives (SPAN), Lingfield, Surrey

Printed and bound in Italy

British Library Cataloguing in Publication Data

Blyton, Enid
        The enchanted sea and other tales.
        I. Title   II. Scholes, Francis
        823'.912[J]   PZ7

ISBN 0 09 167200 7

Enid Blyton's

THE
ENCHANTED SEA

—— **and other tales** ——

Illustrated by

Richard Hook

Hutchinson
London   Melbourne   Auckland   Johannesburg

THE ENCHANTED SEA

ONE lovely sunny morning John and Lucy went out to play in their garden. It was a very big one, and at the end was a broad field.

'Let's go and play in the field this morning!' said Lucy. So down the garden they ran and opened the gate in the wall, meaning to run out into the green field.

But oh, what a surprise! There was no field there! Instead there was the blue sea – and how Lucy and John stared and stared!

'Lucy! What's happened?' asked John, rubbing his eyes. 'Yesterday our field was here. Today there's a big sea!'

'We must be dreaming,' said Lucy. 'Let's pinch each other, John, and if we each feel the pinch, we'll know we're not dreaming.'

So they each pinched one another hard.

'Ooh!' they both cried. 'Stop! You're hurting!'

'It's not a dream, it's real,' said John, rubbing his arm. 'But oh, Lucy! It must be magic or something. Let's go and tell Mummy.'

They were just going to run back to the house when Lucy pointed to something on the smooth blue water.

'Look!' she said. 'There's a boat coming – but isn't it a funny one!'

John looked. Yes, sure enough, it was a boat, a very

strange one. It had high pointed ends, and at one end was a cat's head in wood and at the other a dog's head. A yellow sail billowed out in the wind.

'Who's in the boat?' said John. 'It looks to me like a brownie or gnome, Lucy.'

'I feel a bit frightened,' said Lucy. 'Let's hide behind our garden wall, John, and peep over the top where the pear tree is.'

They ran behind the wall, climbed the pear tree and then, hidden in its leafy branches, peeped over the top. They saw the boat come nearer and nearer, and at last it reached the shore. Out jumped the brownie, threw a rope round a wooden post near by, and then ran off into the wood to the left of the children's garden.

'Well, that was one of the fairy folk for certain!' said John, in excitement. 'Did you see his pointed hat and shoes and his long beard, Lucy?'

For a long time the children watched, but the little gnome did not come back. After a bit John began to long to see the boat more closely, so he and Lucy climbed down the pear tree and ran quietly over the grass to where the boat lay rocking gently.

'Oh, Lucy, it must be a magic one!' said John. 'Do let's get in it just for a moment to see what it feels like! Think how grand it will be to tell everyone we have sat in a brownie's boat!'

So the two children clambered into the little boat and sat down on the wooden seat in the middle. And then a dreadful thing happened!

The rope round the post suddenly uncoiled itself and slipped into the boat. The wind blew hard and the yellow sail billowed out. The boat rocked from end to end, and off it went over the strange enchanted sea!

'Ooh!' said Lucy, frightened. 'John! What shall we do? The boat's sailing away with us!'

But John could do nothing. The wind blew them steadily over the water, and their garden wall grew smaller and smaller, the farther away they sailed.

'That brownie will be cross to find his boat gone,' said Lucy, almost crying. 'Where do you suppose it's taking us?'

On and on went the little boat, the dog's head pointing forwards and the cat's head backwards. Lucy looked at the back of the dog's head, and thought that it looked a little like their dog at home.

'I do wish we had our dear old Rover with us,' she said. 'I'm sure he would be a great help.'

To her great surprise the wooden dog's head pricked up its ears and the head turned round and looked at her.

'If you are fond of dogs, I shall be pleased to help you,' it said.

'You did give us a fright!' said John, almost falling off his seat in surprise. 'Are you magic?'

'Yes, and so is the wooden cat over there,' said the dog. 'We're only wooden figure-heads, but there's plenty of good magic about us. You look nice little children, and if you are fond of animals and kind to them, the cat and I will be very glad to help you.'

'Meeow!' said the cat's head, and it turned round and smiled at the two astonished children.

'Well, first of all, can you tell us about this strange sea?' asked John. 'It's never been here before.'

'Oh yes, it has, but usually at night-time when nobody is about to see it,' said the dog. 'It belongs to the Wizard High-Hat. He sent his servant, the brownie Tick-a-tock, to fetch a red-and-yellow toadstool from the wood near your garden and made the sea stretch from his island to there, so that Tick-a-tock could sail quickly there and back.'

'But I expect he lay down and fell asleep,' said the cat. 'He's always doing that. So when you got into the boat, it sailed off with you instead of the brownie. It doesn't know the difference between you, you see.'

'Oh goodness!' said John, in a fright. 'Does that mean it's taking us to the Wizard High-Hat?'

'Yes,' said the dog, 'and he'll be in a fine temper when he sees you instead of the brownie!'

'Whatever shall we do?' said Lucy, looking anxiously round to see if the wizard's island was anywhere in sight.

'Well, we might be able to help you, if you'll just say a spell over us to make us come properly alive when we get to the island,' said the dog. 'If we were a proper dog and cat we could perhaps protect you.'

'What is the spell?' asked John.

'One of you must stroke my head, and the other must pat the cat's head,' said the dog, looking quite excited. The cat mewed loudly and blinked her green eyes. 'Then you must say the magic word I'll whisper into your ear, and stamp seven times on the bottom of the boat. Then you'll see what happens when we reach the shore. Don't do any of these things till we reach the island.'

The dog whispered the magic word into each child's ear, and they repeated it again and again to themselves to make sure they had it right. Then suddenly Lucy pointed in front of the boat.

'Look!' she said. 'There's the island – and, oh my! Is that the wizard's palace on that hill in the middle?'

'Yes,' said the dog. 'You'll see some of his soldiers in a minute. They always meet the boat.'

Sure enough the children saw six little soldiers come marching out of the palace gates towards the shore. They were dressed in red, and looked very like John's wooden soldiers at home.

The boat sailed nearer and nearer to the shore, and the dog told John and Lucy to use the spell he had taught them. So John stroked the dog's head, Lucy patted the cat's head, and each of them said the magic word, and then stamped loudly on the bottom of the boat seven times.

And what a surprise they had! Each wooden head grew legs and a body, and hey presto, a live cat and dog jumped down from the ends of the boat and frisked round the children in delight!

'We're real, we're real!' they cried.
'Now we can go with
you and help you.'

The boat grounded on the sandy shore and the rope flew out and tied itself round a post. The chief of the soldiers stepped up and looked most astonished to see the two children.

'Where's Tick-a-tock the brownie?' he asked, sternly. 'What are you doing here?'

'Well, you see, we stepped into the brownie's boat and it sailed off with us,' said John. 'We're very sorry, and please would you ask the wizard to excuse us and send the boat back to our garden to take us home again?'

'You must come and ask him yourself,' said the soldier. 'You are very naughty children!'

The six soldiers surrounded John and Lucy and marched them off towards the palace on the hill. The dog and cat followed behind, and the soldiers took no notice of them.

Soon the children were mounting the long flight of steps up to the castle, and were pushed into a large hall, where sat the Wizard High-Hat on a silver throne. He looked most surprised when he saw John and Lucy, and at once demanded to know how they got there.

John told him, and he frowned.

'Now that is most annoying,' he said crossly. 'I want to send my sea to another place tomorrow, and that means that Tick-a-tock won't get back with the toadstool. I shall keep you prisoner here for a hundred years, unless you can do the things I tell you to do.'

Lucy began to cry, and John turned pale.

'Please don't set us very hard tasks,' he said. 'I'm only eight years old, and Lucy's only seven, and doesn't know her six times table yet.'

The wizard laughed scornfully, and commanded his soldiers to take the children to the bead-room. They were led to a small room with a tiny window set high up. On the floor were thousands and thousands of beads of all colours and sizes.

'Now,' said the wizard, 'your first task is to sort out all these beads into their different colours and sizes. You can have today and tonight to do this in, and if you haven't finished by tomorrow morning you shall be my prisoners for a hundred years.'

With that he closed the door with a bang, and he and his soldiers tramped away. The children looked at one another in dismay.

'We can never do that!' said Lucy, in despair. 'Why, it would take us weeks to sort out all these beads!'

'Where are the cat and dog?' asked John, looking all round. 'They don't seem to be here. They might have helped us.'

Suddenly the door opened again, and the dog and cat were flung into the room, panting. Then the door closed again, and the four were prisoners.

'We thought we wouldn't be able to get to you!' said the dog. 'So I bit a soldier on the leg and the cat scratched another on the hand, and they were so angry that they threw us in here with you!'

'Just see what we've got to do!' said Lucy, in despair, and she pointed to the beads. 'We've got to sort out all these before tomorrow morning.'

'My word!' said the dog, blowing out his whiskered cheeks. 'That's a dreadful job! Come, Puss! Let's all set to work.'

The four began to sort out the beads, and for an hour they worked steadily. Then the door opened and a soldier put a loaf of bread, a bone, a jug of water and a saucer of milk into the room. Then the door shut and the key was turned.

The children ate the bread and drank the water. The dog gnawed the bone and the cat drank the milk.

'It's no use going on with these beads,' said the cat, suddenly. 'We shall never get them done. I know what I'll do!'

'What?' asked the children, excitedly.

'You wait and see!' said the cat, and she finished her milk. Then she washed herself. After that she went round the little room, and looked very hard at every hole in the wall.

'Now watch!' she said. She sat down in the middle of the floor and began to make a curious squeaking noise that sounded like a thousand mice squealing at once – and a very curious thing happened!

Out of the mouse holes round the room there came running hundreds of little brown mice. They scampered to where the cat sat, and made ring after ring round her. When about a thousand mice were there, the cat stopped making the curious noise and glared at the mice.

'I could eat you all!' she said, in a frightening voice. 'But if you will do something for me, I will set you free!'

She pointed to the beads. 'Sort those out into their different colours and sizes!' she said. 'And be quick about it!'

At once the thousand mice scuttled to the beads. Each mouse chose a bead of a certain colour and size and carefully put it to start a pile. Soon the little piles grew and grew, and the big pile sank to nothing. In half an hour all the thousands of beads were neatly sorted out into hundreds of piles of beads, all of different colours and sizes.

'Good!' said the cat to the trembling mice. 'You may go!'

Off scampered the mice to their holes and disappeared. The children hugged the clever cat, and thanked her.

'Now we'll let the wizard know his task is done!' said the cat. 'Kick the door, John.'

John kicked the door and an angry soldier opened it.

'Tell the wizard we've finished our work,' said John, and the soldier gaped in astonishment to see the neat piles of beads. He fetched the wizard, who could hardly believe his eyes

'Take them to the Long Field!' said High-Hat to his soldiers. So the children, followed by the cat and dog, were taken to a great field which was surrounded on all sides by high fences. The grass in this field was very long, almost up to the children's knees.

'Here is a pair of scissors for each of you,' said the wizard, with a cunning smile. 'Cut this grass for me before morning, or I will keep you prisoner for a hundred years!'

The children looked at the scissors in dismay. They were very small, and the grass was so long and there was such a lot of it! The wizard and his soldiers shut the gate of the field and left the four alone together.

'Well, I don't know what we're going to do this time!' said John, beginning to cut the grass with his scissors, 'but it seems to me we're beaten!'.

He and Lucy cut away for about an hour, but at the end of that time their hands were so tired, and they had cut so small a patch of grass that they knew it was of no use going on. They would never even get a tenth of the field cut by the morning.

'Can't you think of something clever to help us again?' asked John at last, turning to the cat and dog.

'We're both thinking hard,' said the cat. 'I believe the dog has an idea. Don't disturb him for a minute.'

The dog was lying down, frowning. Lucy and John kept very quiet. Suddenly the dog jumped up and ran to Lucy.

'Feel round my collar,' he said to her. 'You'll find a little wooden whistle there.'

Lucy soon found the whistle, and the dog put it into his mouth. Then he began to whistle very softly. The sound was like the wind in the grass, the drone of bees and the tinkling of faraway water.

Suddenly, holes appeared in the earth all around the high fence, and hundreds of grey rabbits peeped out of them. They had dug their way into the field under the fence, and as soon as they saw the dog blowing on his magic whistle, they ran up to him and sat down in rings round him. He took the whistle from his mouth and looked at them.

'I chase rabbits!' he said. 'But I will let you go free if you will do something for me. Do you see this beautiful green juicy grass? Eat it as quickly as you can, and you shall go the way you came.'

At once the rabbits set to work nibbling the green grass. It was very delicious and they enjoyed it. In an hour's time the whole field was as smooth as velvet, and not a blade of grass was longer than Lucy's little finger.

'Good!' said the dog to the rabbits. 'You may go!'

At once they scampered away. John ran to the gate in the fence and hammered on it. The wizard himself opened it, and when he saw the smooth field, with all the long grass gone, he gasped in astonishment.

'Where's the grass you cut?' he asked at last, looking here and there.

The children didn't know what to say, so they didn't answer. The wizard grew angry, and called his soldiers.

'Take them to the top most room of my palace and lock them in!' he roared. 'They have been using magic! Well, they'll find themselves somewhere they can't use magic now!'

In half a minute the soldiers surrounded the children and animals again and hustled them back to the palace.

Up hundreds and hundreds of stairs they took them, and at last, right at the very top, they came to a room that was locked. The wizard took a key from his girdle and unlocked the door. The children and animals were pushed inside and the door was locked on the outside.

By this time it was almost night-time. A tiny lamp burnt high up in the ceiling. There was one window, but it was barred across. John looked round in despair.

'Well, I don't see what we can do now!' he said, with a sigh. 'I'm afraid, cat and dog, that even you, clever though you are, can't do anything to help us.'

The dog and cat prowled all round the room, but the walls were strong and thick, and the door was locked fast. For a long time the four sat on the floor together, then suddenly the cat jumped up and ran to the window.

'Open it!' she said. 'I want to see if I can squeeze through the bars.'

Lucy and John opened the heavy window, and the cat jumped lightly on to the ledge.

'What's the good of squeezing through the bars?' asked John, peering down. 'You could never jump down, Puss! Why, we're right at the very top of the palace!'

The cat squeezed through the bars and stood on the outer window ledge. Her green eyes shone in the darkness.

'There's another window ledge near by!' she whispered. 'I will jump on to that, and see if the window there is open. If it is, I'll go in, and see if I can find some way of helping you all to escape!'

With that she jumped neatly to the next window ledge, and disappeared. The window there was open and the brave cat leapt lightly into the room. The palace was in darkness. Wizard, soldiers and servants were all sleeping. The soft-footed cat ran down the stairs, and at last reached a room from which loud snores came. She ran in, and by the light of a small candle saw the wizard asleep on his bed. On the table near the candle lay his keys!

In a trice the cat had them in her mouth and back she went up the stairs, leapt on to the window ledge, and then jumped on to the next ledge, mewing to the children as she jumped. How excited they were to see the keys!

John fitted them one by one into the lock of the door until he found the right one. He turned it, and the door opened! Quietly the two children, the cat and the dog slipped down the hundreds of stairs and undid the heavy palace door. Out they went into the moonlight, and ran down to the seashore.

'I do hope the sea still stretches to our garden wall,' said John. 'Hurry up, little boat, and take us home again.'

The boat set off over the water. Suddenly Lucy gave a cry and pointed to each end of the boat. The dog and cat had disappeared, and once more the two wooden figure-heads stood high at each end.

'The magic is gone from them!' said Lucy. 'Oh, I do hope they don't mind. They're gone back to wooden heads again.'

'Don't you worry about us,' said the dog. 'We've enjoyed our adventure, and we're quite happy. I only hope the boat will take you home again.'

On and on sailed the little ship in the bright moonlight. After a long time John caught Lucy's arm and pointed.

'Our garden wall!' he said, in delight.

'Who's that on the edge of the sea?' asked Lucy, seeing a little figure standing there.

'It must be Tick-a-tock the brownie!' said John. 'How pleased he will be to see his boat coming back again. I expect he thought he was quite lost.'

The boat touched the grass, and the children jumped out. They called good-bye to the dog and cat, and then felt themselves pushed aside. The brownie had rushed up to his boat, and leapt in as quickly as he could. The sails filled out and off went the boat in the moonlight, the dog barking and the cat mewing in farewell.

'That's the end of a most exciting adventure,' said John. 'Goodness, I wonder what Mummy has been thinking all this time! We'll tell her all about our adventure, and in the morning perhaps Daddy will make us a raft and we can all go exploring on the magic sea.'

Mummy was glad to see them. She had been so worried. She could hardly believe her ears when she heard all that had happened.

'You must go to bed now,' she said. 'But tomorrow we'll all go down to see the enchanted water, and perhaps Daddy will sail off to the wizard's island to punish him for keeping you prisoner.'

But in the morning the sea was gone! Not a single sign of it was left – there were only green fields and hills stretching far away into the distance. The wizard had called his sea back again, and although John and Lucy have watched for it to return every single day, it never has. Isn't it a pity?

THE GOLDFISH THAT GREW

HOPPETTY had a goldfish in a glass bowl, the prettiest little thing you could wish to see, and the pixie was very proud of it indeed. But what puzzled him was that it didn't grow! It kept as small as could be, and Hoppetty became quite worried about it.

'I give it plenty of good food,' he said, 'and it has a nice piece of green water-weed in the globe, and a little black water-snail for company. I do wonder why it doesn't grow.'

But nobody could tell him why.

'Perhaps it isn't very happy,' said Mrs Biscuit, the baker's wife. 'I've heard it said that unhappy creatures never grow much.'

Hoppetty couldn't bear to think that.

'I'm very kind to it,' he thought. 'It ought to be happy. How dreadful if people should think it doesn't grow because I'm unkind to it and make it unhappy!'

He gave the fish more food than ever, but it wouldn't eat it. The water-snail feasted on it instead, and that made Hoppetty cross. He really didn't know what to do!

Then one day, as he walked over Bumble-Bee Common, he saw a pointed hat sticking up among the gorse bushes, and he knew a witch was somewhere near by. Hoppetty peeped to see.

Yes, sure enough a witch was there, sitting on the

ground beside a little fire she had made. On it she had placed a kettle, which was boiling merrily. Soon she took it off, and held over the flames a little fish she had caught in the river near by. She meant to have it for her dinner.

The fish was very small and the witch was hungry.

'I could eat a much bigger fish than you!' Hoppetty heard her say to the little dead trout. 'I think I'll make you bigger, and then I shall have a fine meal!'

She laid the fish down on the grass, and waved her hand over it twice. 'Little fish, bigger grow, I shall like you better so!' she chanted, and then said a very magic word that made Hoppetty shiver and shake, it was so full of enchantment. But goodness! How he stared to see what happened next! The little fish began to grow and grow, and presently the witch took it up and held it once more over the flames, smiling to see what a fine meal she had!

A great idea came to Hoppetty. He would run straight home, and say the spell over his little goldfish! Then it really would grow, and everyone would be so surprised.

Off went Hoppetty, never stopping to think that it was wrong to peep and pry and use someone else's spell when they did not know he had heard it. He didn't stop running till he got home, and then he went straight to his little goldfish swimming about in its globe.

He waved his hand over it twice. 'Little fish, bigger grow, I shall like you better so!' he chanted, and then he said the very magic word, though it made him shiver and shake to do so.

All at once the goldfish gave a little leap in the water, and began to grow! How it grew! Hoppetty couldn't believe his eyes! It was soon twice as big as before, and still it went on growing!

'You're big enough now, little fish,' said Hoppetty. 'You can stop growing.'

But the fish didn't! It went on and on getting bigger and bigger, and soon it was too big for the bowl.

'Oh dear!' said Hoppetty, in dismay. 'This is very awkward. I'd better fetch my washing-up bowl and put you in that.'

He popped the fish in his washing-up bowl, but still it went on growing, and Hoppetty had to put it into his bath.

'Please, please stop!' he begged the fish. 'You're far too big, really!'

But the fish went on growing, and soon it was too big for the bath. Then Hoppetty really didn't know what to do.

'I'd better take my fish under my arm and go and find that old witch!' he said at last. 'She can tell me how to stop my goldfish from getting any bigger. Oh dear, I do hope she won't be cross!'

He picked the goldfish up, and wrapped a wet handkerchief round its head so that it wouldn't die, and set off to Bumble-Bee Common. How heavy the fish was! And it kept getting heavier and heavier too, because it went on growing. Hoppetty staggered along the road with it, and everyone stared at him in surprise. Then a gnome policeman tapped him on the arm.

'You are being cruel to that fish,' he said. 'He is panting for breath, poor thing. Put him in that pond over there at once.'

Sure enough the wet handkerchief had slipped off the fish's head, and it was opening and shutting its mouth in despair. It wriggled and struggled, and Hoppetty could hardly hold it. He went to the pond and popped it in. It slid into the water, flicked its great tail and sent a wave right over Hoppetty's feet.

Then who should come by but that witch! Hoppetty ran to her and told her all that had happened, begging her to forgive him for using her spell.

'Do you mean to say that you were peeping and prying on me?' said the witch in a rage. 'Well it just serves you right, you nasty little pixie! Your fish can go on growing till it's bigger than the town itself, and that will be a fine punishment for you!'

'Madam, tell the spell that will make the fish go back to its right size,' said the policeman, sternly. 'Hoppetty has done wrong, but you cannot refuse his request now that he has asked your pardon.'

The witch had to obey. She went to the pond and waved her hand over it twice. 'Big fish, smaller grow, I shall like you better so!' she chanted, and then she said another magic word. At once the great goldfish shrank smaller and smaller, and at last it was its own size again. Hoppetty cried out in delight, and ran to get a net to catch it.

But that little fish wouldn't be caught! It wasn't going to go back into a tiny glass globe again now that it had a whole pond to swim about in, and frogs and stickle-backs, snails and beetles to talk to. Oh no!

Hoppetty had to give it up and he went sadly back home.

'I've lost my little fish,' he said, 'but it serves me right for peeping and prying. I shan't do that again!'

And I don't believe he ever did!

THE GOBLIN IN THE TRAIN

A LL the toys in the playroom were most excited. Tomorrow the clockwork train was going to take them to a pixie party, and what fun that would be.

But, oh dear, wasn't it a shame, when Andrew was playing with the train that day, he overwound it and broke the spring. Then it wouldn't go, and all the toys crowded round it that night, wondering what they would do the next night when they wanted to go to the party.

'I'm very, very sorry,' said the clockwork train. 'But I simply can't move a wheel, you know. My spring is quite broken. You won't be able to go to the pixie party, because I can't take you. It's all Andrew's fault.'

'Well, he must have broken your spring by accident,' said the rag doll. 'He's very careful with us, generally. But it is dreadfully disappointing.'

'Couldn't we send a message to the little goblin who lives under the holly bush?' said the teddy-bear. 'He is very clever at mending things, and he might be able to mend the broken spring.'

'Good idea!' cried the toys, and they at once sent a message to the goblin. He came in five minutes, and shook his head when he saw the broken spring.

'This will take me a long time to mend,' he said. 'I doubt if I'll get it done by cock-crow.'

'Please, please try!' cried the toys. So he set to work. He had all sorts of weird tools, not a bit like ours, and he worked away as hard as ever he could. And suddenly, just as he had almost finished, a cock crew! That meant that all toys and fairy folk must scuttle away to their own places again, but the little goblin couldn't bear to leave his job unfinished.

'I'll just pop into the cab of the train,' he called to the toys. 'I'll make myself look like a little driver, and as Andrew knows the spring is broken, perhaps he won't look at the train today or notice me. Then I can quickly finish my work tonight and you'll be able to go to the party!'

The toys raced off to their cupboard, thinking how very kind the goblin was. He hopped into the cab, sat down there, and kept quite still, just as if he were a little boy driver.

Andrew didn't once look at his engine that day, and the toys were so glad. When night came again the goblin set to work, and very soon he had finished mending the spring. He wound up the engine, and hey presto, its wheels went round and it raced madly round the playroom.

'Good! Good!' cried the toys. 'Now we can go to the party! Hurrah! What can we do to return your kindness, goblin?'

'Well,' said the goblin, turning rather red, 'there is one thing I'd like. You know, I'm rather an ugly little chap, and I've never been asked to a pixie party in my life. I suppose you wouldn't take me with you? If you could, I'd drive the train, and see that nothing went wrong with it.'

'Of course, of course!' shouted the toys in glee. 'You shall come with us goblin, and we'll tell all the pixies how nice you are!'

Then they all got into the train, the goblin wound it up again, and they went to the party. What a glorious time they had, and what a hero the goblin was when the toys had finished telling everyone how he had mended the broken train!

He drove them all safely back again to the playroom and then, dear me, he was so happy and so tired that he fell fast asleep sitting in the cab!

And in the morning Andrew found him there and was so surprised.

'Look, Mummy, look!' he shouted. 'The train has suddenly got a driver, and goodness me, the spring is mended too! Isn't that a strange thing! And isn't he a nice little driver, Mummy? Wherever could he have come from?'

But Mummy couldn't think how he could have got there.

'He must have been there all the time and you didn't notice him before,' she said.

'No, Mummy, really,' said Andrew. 'I've often wished my clockwork train had a driver, and I know I should have noticed him if he had been here before. Oh, I do hope he stays. He looks so nice and real.'

The goblin was so happy to find that Andrew liked him and was pleased with him. But he was happier still that night when all the toys crowded round him and begged him to stay and be one of them.

'We like you very much,' they said. 'Don't go back to your holly bush, but stay here and be the driver of Andrew's train. We'll have such fun together every night!'

The goblin wanted nothing better than to stay where he was, for he had often been very lonely under his holly bush.

'I'd love to stay!' he said. 'Come on, I'll take you for a fine ride round and round the playroom!' The toys almost woke Andrew up with their shouts of delight.

Andrew is very proud of his train-driver. He shows him to everyone, and I do hope you'll see him for yourself some day. Then perhaps you can tell Andrew the story of how he got there.

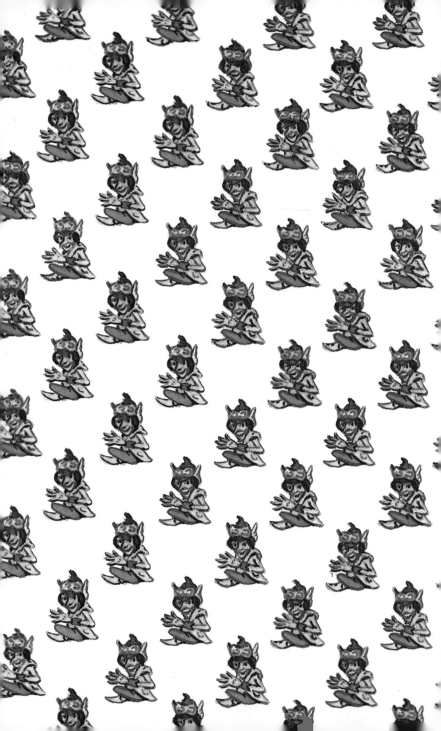